TITCHY
WITCH
AND THE SCARY HAIRCUT

For Austin
R.I.

For Edie, who has the best red hair ever!
K.M.

ORCHARD BOOKS
338 Euston Road
London NW1 3BH
Orchard Books Australia
Level 17/207 Kent Street, Sydney, NSW 2000

First published in Great Britain in 2013
First paperback publication 2014
ISBN 978 1 40830 713 7 (HB)
ISBN 978 1 40830 717 5 (PB)

A CIP catalogue record for this book is available from the British Library

1 3 5 7 9 10 8 6 4 2 (HB)
1 3 5 7 9 10 8 6 4 2 (PB)
Printed in China

Orchard Books is a division of Hachette Children's Books, an Hachette UK company.
www.hachette.co.uk

Titchy Witch and the Scary Haircut

BY ROSE IMPEY ILLUSTRATED BY KATHARINE McEWEN

ORCHARD

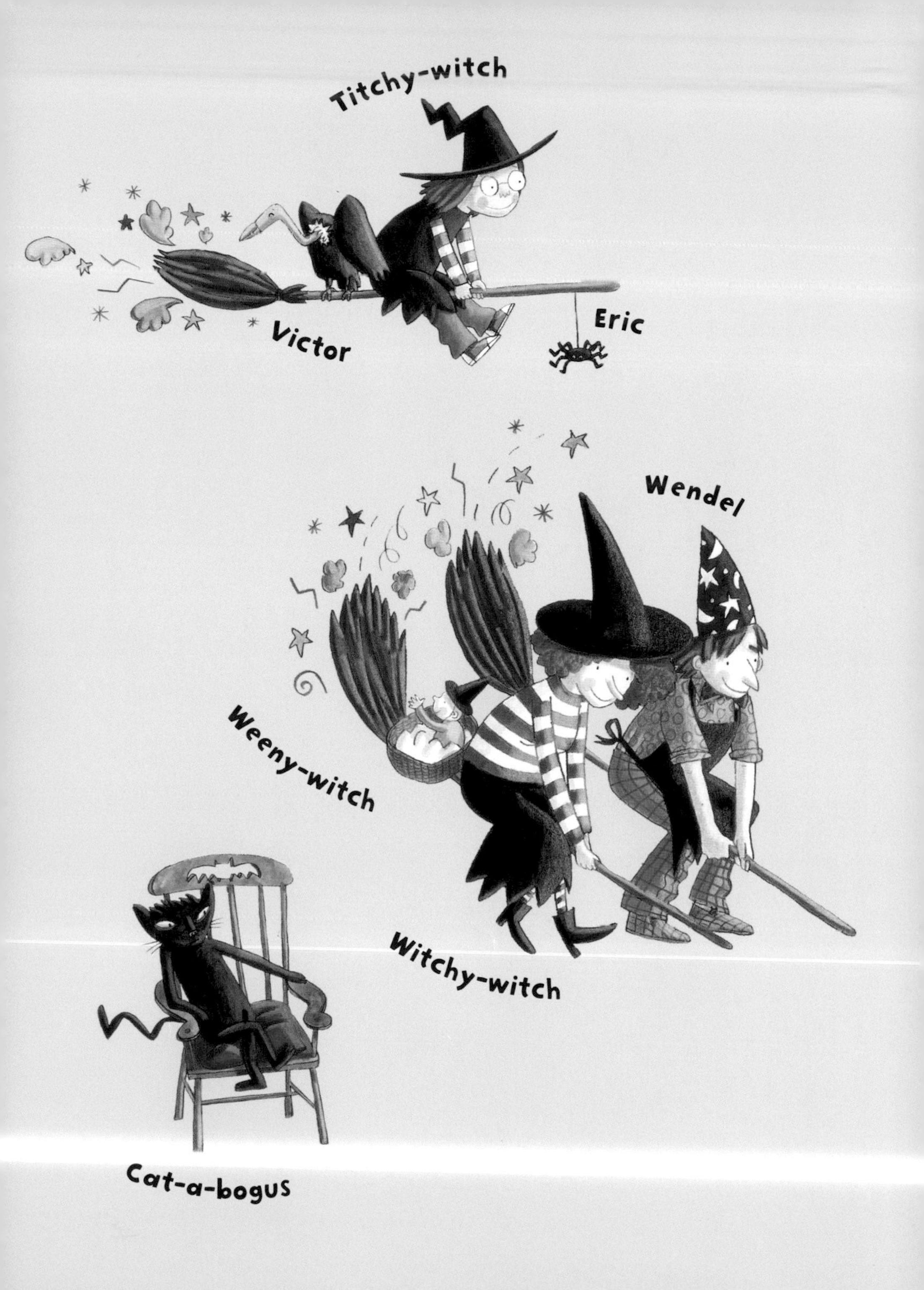
Titchy-witch
Victor
Eric
Wendel
Weeny-witch
Witchy-witch
Cat-a-bogus

Titchy-witch was proud of her red hair.
"A very special colour for a little witch," Mum told her.

And now that she was seven witch years old, it was time for her first proper haircut.

Titchy-witch was very excited...

...until she realised that
Cat-a-bogus would be taking her.
Titchy-witch thought the cat was
too bossy.

"What can I do-oo for you-oo?"
asked Mr Barn-Owl, the barber.
"A haircut," said Cat-a-bogus.
"And make it very short, please."

Titchy-witch didn't like the sound of that.

But Mr Barn-Owl swivelled his head and gave her a friendly wink.

Titchy-witch was too small to see
in the mirror.
But she could hear the *snip-snap*
of the scissors.

And she could see *lots* of hair
falling on the floor.

When Mr Barn-Owl asked,
"Will that do-oo?"
Cat-a-bogus shook his head.
"Shorter, please!" he said.

Finally the cat purred, "Perrrrfect."
Titchy-witch didn't think it was perfect.

She thought it was the shortest haircut she had ever seen.

Gobby-goblin and his brother thought it was the *funniest* haircut they had ever seen.

Titchy-witch went home in a terrible temper.

"I need a spell," she told Dido.
"A hair-raising spell!"
Uh-oh, thought the little dragon.
That sounded like trouble.

It was certainly a very *hairy* spell:

Hair of bears and fleece of sheep,
Giant's beard plucked in his sleep,
Weave together, then...hey, presto!
In double-quick time make my hair grow...

Witchy-witch was puzzled. She had to trim Titchy-witch's fringe three times before supper.

"Having your hair cut seems to have made it grow faster," she said.

But Cat-a-bogus knew what was going on.

"Don't worry," he told Witchy-witch. "We'll go back to Mr Barn-Owl in the morning and get it cut again."

Oh, no! Titchy-witch didn't want to go back to the barber. At least, not with Cat-a-bogus.

She needed another spell – and fast!

This time she needed a spell to *stop* her hair from growing.

But, as usual, Titchy-witch was in such a hurry she didn't *stop* to think first.

Bald eagle's egg
and fruit bat's ear,
Make this stupid
hair disappear!

Titchy-witch thought the spell had worked quite well – until she looked in a mirror. The spell had worked *a bit too well.*

All her hair was gone and now her head looked like a shiny egg.

Suddenly they heard Cat-a bogus coming.
Titchy-witch grabbed her hat and jumped into bed.

Titchy-witch pretended to be asleep, but Cat-a-bogus wasn't fooled. "Since when do little witches go to bed with their hats on?" he asked, plucking it off.

“Please don’t make me go back to the barber’s,” Titchy-witch begged.

Cat-a-bogus was bossy, but he wasn't mean. He made a deal with Titchy-witch. If she promised not to do any more magic, he would make her hair come back.

The cat purred a magic spell under his breath:

Abracadabra! Wind, hail, snow and rain!
Make Titchy-witch's hair grow again!

Right up until she fell asleep,
Titchy-witch managed to keep her
promise not to do any more magic.

But tomorrow...well, that might be a little bit harder.

BY ROSE IMPEY ILLUSTRATED BY KATHARINE McEWEN

Enjoy a little more magic with all the Titchy-witch tales:

- ❑ Titchy-witch and the Birthday Broomstick
- ❑ Titchy-witch and the Disappearing Baby
- ❑ Titchy-witch and the Frog Fiasco
- ❑ Titchy-witch and the Stray Dragon
- ❑ Titchy-witch and the Bully-Boggarts
- ❑ Titchy-witch and the Wobbly Fang
- ❑ Titchy-witch and the Get-Better Spell
- ❑ Titchy-witch and the Magic Party
- ❑ Titchy-witch and the Teacher-Charming Spell
- ❑ Titchy-witch and the Scary Haircut
- ❑ Titchy-witch and the Babysitting Spell
- ❑ Titchy-witch and the Forbidden Forest